ABBY & HOLLY SERIES, BOOK 3

I0662749

Secrets of the Trunk

JANICE SPINA

Illustrations & Cover by John Spina

1

COPYRIGHT 2019
By Janice Spina

Published by Janice Spina 2019

Library of Congress Control Number: 2019911972

This book is a work of fiction. Any references to persons, places or things are purely coincidental. Names, characters, places and events are products of this author's imagination.

DEDICATION

To my granddaughter, Leah, who loves to read about mysteries, adventures and everything that is creative

ACKNOWLEDGEMENTS

Thank you to my beta readers, Patricia Bradley, Michelle Clement James, Michele Rolfe, and Frances Stewart for their tireless efforts to read and review this book and for their helpful input. Their assistance is invaluable and appreciated.

A special thank you to my husband, John, for the lovely chapter illustrations and the beautiful cover of this book.

OTHER BOOKS BY JANICE SPINA:
<u>Pre-School to Grade Three:</u>

Louey the Lazy Elephant

Ricky the Rambunctious Raccoon

Jerry the Crabby Crayfish
(Pinnacle Book Achievement Award)

Lamby the Lonely Lamb
(Silver Medal from Mom's Choice Awards)

Jesse the Precocious Polar Bear

Broose the Moose on the Loose
(Pinnacle Book Achievement Award)

Sebastian Meets Marvin the Monkey

Colby the Courageous Cat
(Pinnacle Book Achievement Award)

Jeffrey the Jittery Giraffe
(Pinnacle Book Achievement Award)

Clarence Henry the Hermit Crab

Lucy the Talented Toy Terrier

Middle-Grade/Preteen/YA:

The Case of the Missing Cell Phone

(Davey & Derek Junior Detectives Series, Book 1)

(Pinnacle Book Achievement Award & Reader's Favorite Book Awards – Honorable Mention)

The Case of the Mysterious Black Cat

(Davey & Derek Junior Detectives Series, Book 2)

(Pinnacle Book Achievement Award)

The Case of the Magical Ivory Elephant

(Davey & Derek Junior Detectives Series, Book 3)

(Pinnacle Book Achievement Award & Silver Medal from Reader's Favorite Book Awards)

The Case of the Brown Scraggly Dog

(Davey & Derek Junior Detectives Series, Book 4)

(Finalist in Red City Review Book Awards)

The Case of the Sad Mischievous Ghost

(Davey & Derek Junior Detectives Series, Book 5)

(Pinnacle Book Achievement Award & Silver Medal from Authorsdb Cover Contest)

The Case of the Mystery of the Bells

*Davey & Derek Junior Detectives,
Book 6*

(Pinnacle Book Achievement Award)

Abby & Holly Series Book 1,

School Dance

(Pinnacle Book Achievement Award)

*Abby & Holly Series, Book 2,
Unfortunate Events*

(Pinnacle Book Achievement Award)

<u>Novels: (under J.E. Spina)</u>

Hunting Mariah

(Finalist in Authorsdb First Lines Contest)

How Far Is Heaven

An Angel Among Us (A Short Story Collection)

Mariah's Revenge (Sequel to Hunting Mariah)

(Finalist in Authorsdb First Lines Contest)

Table of Contents

INTRODUCTION

This is **Book 3** of the **Abby & Holly Series**: This book deals with secrets from an old trunk and imparts the message family and friends are important and that with their love and support there is no obstacle you cannot overcome.

This Series is a spin-off from **Davey & Derek Junior Detective Series, Book 5, The Case of the Sad Mischievous Ghost.**

Abby and Holly, first cousins on their mothers' side, first appeared in **Book 5** of the **Davey & Derek Series** when they enlisted the twins' help to capture some ghosts that inhabited Abby Rizzo's house.

There is one ghost that has returned to haunt their house. Her name is Felicity. She has become the protector of Abby and Holly and refuses to leave until she feels the cousins don't need her anymore.

A second ghost, Minerva, has come to stay with Felicity. Minerva was unwanted in her home where she had once lived and continued to haunt after her death. The new owners of her home drove her out with the help of a ghost hunter. Minerva was welcomed to come and live with them by Felicity and the girls.

Holly Lester is living with her cousin Abby and her family until Holly's father returns from a business trip overseas. When he returns, Holly's parents will have to find a home of their own or live with the Rizzo's until they do.

Abby has long brown hair and green eyes. She wants to be a fashion designer one day. Holly has long blonde tresses and blue eyes. She wants to be an author and write all kinds of mysteries.

Now the girls are in their own series doing what girls like to do. They have their own adventures, solve mysteries, and intcract with the twins, Davey and Derek Donato, from time to time.

Book 1, Abby & Holly, School Dance deals with a bully and how the girls handle the situation.

Book 2 Abby & Holly Series: Unfortunate Events touches on unexpected incidents and how to overcome disappointments in life. Another ghost, Minerva, is introduced in this book.

These middle-grade books carry life lessons that encourage children, preteens, and young adults to be kind, caring and sensitive to others' feelings. The characters show respect toward one another and are polite to their parents and others. I will never have any offensive language or subject matter in these stories.

Watch for book 4 coming later in 2019 with a new adventure for the girls.

CHAPTER ONE

A Surprise Discovery

Abby and Holly were looking forward to a long summer vacation now that school was out. They knew their mothers had plans for them to help around the house but the girls had their own plans too.

Two of their chores were to clean out the basement and the library/den that was lined with old books that came with the house when it was purchased.

Abby's father had wanted to throw all of the books away after they had moved in. But Abby begged him to let her look them over before he did. However, she hadn't yet done this and it was now time to clear them out per her father's request.

Abby pulled down some of the books on the lower shelves on the right while Holly worked on the left side of the room. There were rolling ladders that were attached up at the highest racks in order to reach the upper shelves.

Holly was sitting on the bottom step of the ladder when she suddenly decided to climb up to the middle and pull the ladder along for a ride. She disturbed some dust and debris which came flying down around her cousin.

"Holly, what're you doing? I'm getting covered with dust and stuff," Abby hollered.

"Oops, sorry, Abby! This is so much fun. I was getting tired of looking at these old dusty books. Give it a try."

"Okay," Abby jumped up on her ladder and pulled herself along the opposite way.

"Wow, this is fun, Holly!"

The girls were unaware of a cloud of dust as it swirled in a circle at the bottom of the ladders. It settled down after a few minutes and landed on the coffee table in the middle of the room.

Holly and Abby hopped off the ladders and went back to looking over the books. The dust rose from the table and stayed up in the air in front of the girls.

"What is that, Holly?"

"I don't know. Is it another ghost?" Holly said with a quiver in her voice.

"Look, it's moving to the wall and going into the hidden passageways. Let's follow it to see where it's going," Abby suggested with a lift of her eyebrows.

"No, I don't think so, Abby. We may get stuck in there. We don't know if it is a kind spirit or one that could do us harm."

"Let's ask Felicity. She probably knows what it is."

The girls rushed upstairs to their shared room. Even though Holly did have her own room on the third floor in her parents' apartment the girls preferred to be together in Abby's room. They called out to their ghost friend, Felicity, who inhabited the secret passageway in the wall behind their bed.

"Felicity, do you hear me?" Abby said in a soft whisper.

Holly added, "Felicity, where are you?"

A white figure with flowing hair flew out of the passageway next to their bed and floated in front of the girls.

Did you call me?

"Yes, Felicity. We have a question for you," Abby explained in detail about the dust cloud they had encountered down in the library.

Felicity listened. *I'll have to check it out. You said it went into the passageway in the library? I'll go down there and find out. I'll be back in a second or so.*

"Thanks, Felicity. We'll wait downstairs in the library," Abby said as the girls headed back there.

"What do you think she'll find, Abby?"

"Hmm, I don't know. It could have been just a cloud of dust and not an entity at all," Holly responded with a thoughtful expression.

Before the girls could discuss this subject again Felicity flew into the library and hovered by the passageway.

It's not a ghost, phantom or specter, like me, or whatever you want to call me. It's called a dust sprite. It is not able to communicate in the way I do. It can only float around and settle inside a book or something solid like that. It came from a young girl who read some of these books. It is part of her memory which managed to cling to the books. It will leave now that I spoke to it. It has no place to stay here. The young girl is no longer here.

"Wow, that is strange, Felicity. It's part of the girl's memory that clung to the books she read?" Abby queried.

Yes, that is what I said. Are you my echo? Felicity chuckled.

"Oh no, sorry, I didn't mean to do that, Felicity. I was just surprised to hear of such a thing as a dust sprite."

"Yeah, that is weird, Felicity," Holly added with a quirky expression on her face.

"Does that mean we'll find more of these dust sprites inside all the books on the shelves?" Abby asked in a shaky voice.

No, I don't think so. But if it will make you feel better, I will scan all the books on the shelves quickly to make sure.

"Oh thank you, Felicity. We appreciate that, don't we, Holly?"

"Yes, most definitely!"

Felicity flew up and around the ladders and scanned all the shelves in minutes and settled down in front of the girls who were sitting on the couch now.

There are no more dust sprites in any of the books. All are safe for you.

"Wow, that was quite impressive, Felicity. You did that so fast," Abby proclaimed.

"Thank you, Felicity, for your help. We feel better, right, Abby?"

"Oh yes, thank you, Felicity. Now we can get back to work."

You are both welcome, ladies. I will be available if you need me. Just call. Minerva and I will have something to discuss now with this dust sprite.

Felicity disappeared from view as she floated through the cracks in the passageway on her way up to the girls' bedroom corridor where she had left Minerva, her ghost friend. Minerva had been kicked out by the new occupants of her longtime home in the neighborhood. She was asked to come to live here by Felicity with permission from Abby and Holly, of course. Felicity was happy to have a friend.

Felicity was relieved that the dust sprite had left without too much convincing on her part. She had known dust sprites that could be quite nasty at times. This she didn't tell the girls for fear of frightening them. She would watch over them. After all, that was why she was here. She would only leave if they asked her to go. Until that time she was their caretaker.

CHAPTER TWO

Books and More Books

After a few hours' work, the girls had plenty of books they had chosen to give away, donate or throw away if no one wanted them. Some were old copies of the classics but not in good condition. They probably wouldn't be worth too much, but the girls decided to check that fact out just in case.

There were copies of encyclopedias which the cousins enjoyed scanning through. Holly giggled when she saw some of the old bathing suits that people wore at that time.

"Wow, look at these, Abby! These are ancient! Maybe our great grandmothers wore these."

"Ha, you could be right, Holly. They are strange and so long. Women were well covered up in those days."

"We should ask our mothers about these. Maybe they remember them. What do you think, Abby?"

"Oh boy, I don't want to be the one who asks them. They could be insulted that we think they're that old!" Holly laughed.

"Oh yeah, you're right, Holly. I guess I'll just show them and let them share with us what they know."

"Yep, I think that's the safest way to go, Abby."

"What about these books? What pile do we put them in? They look like someone wrote them in long-hand." Holly studied the books closer with a magnifying glass.

"Let me see," Abby leaned over her cousin's shoulder to get a better look. "Ooh, look at the script. It's beautiful! It looks like calligraphy."

"Let's put these aside to read later. They will make for interesting reading. We can begin boxing up the ones that we're going to take to the library or bookstores. This pile here is the throw-away pile. These books are in bad condition, broken spines, and faded print and torn covers. No one is going to want them," Abby announced.

Holly went out to the garage to get some more boxes to begin the task. The girls worked another hour getting all the books packed and carted out the others to the trash after their mothers checked them out to make sure they were not valuable.

"Great job, girls!" their mothers exclaimed after looking over the several boxes tightly packed to be given away. They noticed the smaller pile on the coffee table and Abby's mother, Jane Rizzo, asked, "What are these books doing here? Are you keeping them?"

"Yes, Mom. They are written by hand in a beautiful calligraphy. Holly and I want to read them before we decide what to do with them."

"They could be valuable, girls. Keep them safe. We'll look them over after you finish. Okay?"

"Sure, we could take them down to that new book store in town. They may know if they are worth something."

"Good idea, girls," Holly's mother, Shirley Lester, added.

"Are you hungry? Why don't you two go upstairs and get cleaned up? We'll prepare lunch," Abby's mother, Jane Rizzo, announced.

CHAPTER THREE

Nighttime Reading

The girls settled down that night to some intriguing reading with the books they had saved from their library. Holly chose two books and Abby had three by her bedside table.

"Hmm, this is interesting," Holly held the page open so that Abby could see it.

"Wow, that is beautiful writing! Look at her name – Annabelle."

"Umm, yes, it is, but that is not what I meant about interesting, Abby. Look closely at the writing and read it."

"Oh, my goodness, it looks like the writing that our ghosts write when they leave messages for us."

"Yes, also, do you understand what this means?"

"Let me see," Abby pulled the book closer and studied the passages. "Yes, I think I do. Do you remember the trunk we found last month? Dad put it back down in the basement."

"Um, yes, I remember. We had a tough time, or should I say, the boys had a difficult time lugging it up the stairs."

"Oh, yeah! It was quite entertaining. The twins were so funny along with their friend Mickey," Holly giggled.

"I thought they were going to explode because their faces were so red!" Abby joined in the chuckles.

"Hey, we should look through the trunk again. This person who is writing keeps talking about the trunk and its secrets. I wonder what that means."

"Maybe there is something valuable in there. We didn't get to empty it out and only took out the old clothes and tried some on. Right afterwards, Mom told us to put it all away."

"I think Aunt Jane was nervous about us trying on other people's clothes. They were a little dusty and yellowed."

"Yeah, I guess you're right, Holly. It gave me the creeps too when we put them on. I was glad to take them off."

"Well, how are we going to get the trunk back upstairs?" Abby put on her thinking expression as she scrunched her eyebrows and pursed her lips.

Holly watched her cousin in thinking mode and couldn't keep from laughing. "What are you doing, Abby?"

"What? Oh, you mean my face. I always do this so I can think better."

"It's pretty weird you know. Have you ever looked in the mirror at yourself?"

"Ah, no. I'm sure it's scary. Sorry about that. I'll have to come up with a new face when I'm trying to think."

"Why do you need a special thinking face, Abby?"

"Oh, I don't know. I read something about when you concentrate you need a facial expression to help you think."

"Really? I never heard of such a thing."

"Well, what kind of face do you make when you are concentrating, Holly?"

"Hmm, I don't know."

Abby laughed out loud when she saw the face that her cousin was displaying at that moment.

"What's so funny, Abby?"

"Well, you just had a weird kind of expression on your face as you were thinking. That must be your thinking face."

Holly jumped out of bed and went to the full-length standing mirror and tried to recreate the face Abby said she had.

"Is this the face you saw, Holly?"

"Not quite. Squint a little more and bite your lip."

"Like this?"

"Yup, that's it! Ha, you got your own weird thinking face too, Holly."

"I guess I do. Oh well, we both better work on more attractive thinking faces for the twins. We don't want to scare them away." The girls giggled and put down their books as their mothers entered their bedroom to say goodnight.

"Everything okay in here, girls?" Their mothers asked as they leaned over and kissed them goodnight and tucked them into their queen-size bed.

"Oh, we're just being silly, Mom. Everything's fine," Abby reassured her mother.

"Yup, we're silly girls, that's all, Mom!" Holly added for her mother.

"Well, get some sleep. We'll see you in the morning. Goodnight, girls."

"Goodnight, Mom and Aunt Shirl."

"Goodnight, Mom and Aunt Jane."

The girls sighed and laid back and closed their eyes with visions of trunks dancing around in their heads.

CHAPTER FOUR

sweep patio
vacuum rugs
wash dishes
set table
do laundry

Chores First

After breakfast, the girls finished up their chores as quickly as possible in order to go downstairs to the basement and check out the trunk. They told their mothers that they were going to clean out some stuff in the basement.

"Really? It's awfully dark and dingy down there. Are you sure you want to do that?" Jane asked with a frown as she looked at her sister, Shirley.

"What do you think you want to clean out down there, girls?" Shirley inquired.

"Well, we might as well explain what we want to do, Holly."

"Right, okay. You tell them, Abby."

Jane and Shirley exchanged questioning glances as they waited for Abby to continue.

Abby explained about the books and what they referred to in the trunks as maybe holding secrets of some kind.

"Secrets? What kind of secrets?" Jane prodded.

"Well, that is what we want to find out," Holly added.

"I see. I think you might want some extra lighting down there though."

"That would be great, Mom. What do you have for us to use?"

"Well, your father has some standup lights that we can bring down. He used them to finish up Aunt Shirl's apartment late at night before he had installed the overhead light fixtures."

"That would be perfect. Are they heavy to carry?"

"Yes, a little. Aunt Shirley and I will carry them down for you. Make sure you are careful down there and call us if you need help."

"Sure thing, Mom. We'll be careful. What trouble can we possibly get into?"

"I don't know, Abby. But you always find a way," her mother chuckled.

The girls noticed the lock on the trunk and tried to pry it open. Abby suddenly rushed upstairs to the desk in the library and pulled out her trusty letter opener and ran back downstairs.

"Where did you go in such a hurry, Abby?"

"I know we can't open it without this." Abby held up her shiny letter opener.

Abby leaned over the trunk and wiggled the letter opener into the keyhole. After a few tries, it didn't open.

She sighed and was about to give up when the lid lifted slightly on its own. She stepped back from it in alarm and looked at Holly, her mother and aunt, who were as surprised as she was at this.

"Well, that was strange. Maybe you did open it with the letter opener, after all, Abby," Holly exclaimed still feeling a little shocked.

"No, I don't think so, Holly. I had already taken it out when it opened by itself," Abby whispered so her mother and aunt wouldn't hear.

Together, the four slowly lifted the lid which was extremely heavy. The mothers set up the lights and left the girls on their own but not before saying, "Be careful, girls. If you need us we'll be in the kitchen."

"Okay, Mom, Aunt Shirley. Thanks for your help," Abby said with some anxiety.

The girls got to work as Holly pulled out all the old clothes that they had previously tried on and set them aside. Underneath the clothes were some gloves, fans and hair ornaments.

Abby picked up one of the gaudy-looking hair clips and tried it in her hair. It was quite ornate and heavy.

"Looks a little too heavy for my taste. It hurt my scalp. I wonder how they wore these things in those days."

"I don't know. I don't like them either, Abby. I prefer our slim designs with little decorations. Plain stuff that clips and holds your hair without pinching or taking out clumps of hair."

"Yeah, me too. Let's keep digging in here and pull out more stuff. There's bound to be something interesting."

At the bottom of the trunk there was a box that looked like the kind you put little keepsakes in, but it had a keyhole. It was faded and the writing was indecipherable. The girls tried to open the lid to look inside.

Abby's eyes popped open wider and she gasped. "Oh my, look at it, Holly!"

The next minute they were both in the dark.

CHAPTER FIVE

Ghostly Discussions

Felicity and Minerva were discussing the dust sprite that the girls had discovered locked inside a book in the library.

What do you think about that dust sprite that appeared to the girls, Felicity?

I don't like it one bit, Minerva. I don't trust it either. I will be keeping an eye out for it in case it decides to come back. I think it wants to cause some mischief.

Why do you think that, Felicity?

Well, I've known a few of those pesky sprites in my lifetime. I know what they are capable of doing. It has been locked up for many years and now wants to cause some trouble.

What are we going to do to prevent it from harming the girls?

Don't worry, Minerva. You get so nervous about everything. You must have been quite a nervous ninny in your day.

I'm sorry, Felicity. I guess I haven't changed after my death. I am still a nervous ninny in a ghost's body.

It's okay, Minerva. I'll take care of everything. You need not worry. Okay?

Okay, Felicity. You are the best friend I ever had. In fact, I think you are the only friend I ever had even if you are a ghost.

Yes, I am that but so are you, my friend.

The two ghosts chittered and hid inside the wall as they heard voices coming into the room.

"Shirley, did you hear that?"

"What, Jane? What did you hear?"

"I thought I heard some voices in here. It couldn't be the girls, they're in the basement."

"I'm sorry, Sis, I didn't hear anything. But your hearing has always been better than mine. I guess I went to too many concerts in my day."

"Maybe we should check on the girls, Shirl. They have been in the basement for a couple of hours now. They must be knee-deep in dust and grime."

"Let's go and see what they have found in the trunk. Maybe they found some treasure?" Shirley chuckled.

"Yeah, who knows? Maybe we'll all be rich."

The phone rang as the mothers were heading to the basement. Jane grabbed it in the library and listened to the caller. She raised her eyebrows toward her sister.

"Yes, I see. Thank you for calling." Jane hung up and looked at Shirley.

"Who was that, Jane?"

"That's very strange. It was someone who said they saw an object coming out of our chimney."

"An object coming out of the chimney? What kind of object?"

"The caller wasn't specific. He said he lives in the area and was walking his dog as something flew out of the chimney in front of him and swiftly disappeared."

"That is weird. Maybe he's a practical joker or something. How did he get your number?"

"Hmm, I didn't ask him. But everyone knows about this house and probably knows our names."

"Yeah, I guess it's easy to find phone numbers as long as you have a name and an address."

"I don't think I'll mention it to Bob. He will think we're as crazy as the caller. He doesn't believe in such things."

"Yes, my husband is like that too. But since I have been here in this house I am becoming a believer in strange things such as ghosts."

"I know what you mean, Shirl. I've seen a ghost or two myself. I worry about the girls though. I hope they haven't found anything…"

Before Jane could finish her sentence a scream was heard coming from the basement.

The women ran to the basement door and yanked it open.

CHAPTER SIX

Moms to the Rescue

The girls were nowhere in sight when their mothers got down to the basement. Jane and Shirley looked around and called out the girls' names.

"Abby, Holly, where are you?"

A banging could be heard from inside the old trunk. The women hurried over to the trunk and tried to lift the lid. It took both of them pulling and tugging for a few minutes before it opened.

"What happened, girls? How did you get stuck in the trunk?" Jane leaned over and helped the girls out.

Abby grasped her mother in a tight hug and said, "Thank you, Mom, for coming to check on us. I don't know how long we would have been able to breathe in there."

Holly hugged her mother and thanked her too for being a worry wort.

"Oh my God, thank goodness we do worry a lot about you two," Jane said as she held tightly to Abby and didn't want to let go.

"How come you couldn't open the trunk from the inside?" Shirley asked as she opened and closed the trunk now without too much effort.

"Hmm, that's strange. It opens up easier now and doesn't feel as heavy," Jane observed.

"I don't know what happened, Mom," Abby answered in a quivering voice. "One minute I was looking at something glowing and the next minute I was inside the trunk with Holly."

"You said it was glowing?" Shirley asked.

"Yeah. It was glowing like a blue light. Also, I felt as if someone pushed me inside after Abby fell in."

"What do you mean you felt someone push you?" Shirley quizzed in alarm.

"Yeah, I felt someone's hands on my back when I was leaning in to look at what Abby told me she had found. The next minute I was inside the dark trunk next to her."

"All right. That settles it, girls. No more basement for you and no more looking inside this trunk. I can't keep an eye on you 24-7, you know. Please stay away from it until I can have your father check it over to make sure it doesn't close on you again. It's a dead subject."

"Okay, Mom. I don't think I want to look at it anymore. It was scary being inside it."

"Yeah, I didn't think we would be able to get out. What if you didn't come and check on us, Mom and Aunt Jane?"

"We were on our way down when the phone rang and then we heard your screams," Jane explained

"You heard our screams? We didn't scream because it happened too quickly to react," Abby cried in alarm.

"We did scream afterward and banged the inside of the lid, when we heard you calling us, until you opened it," Holly exclaimed.

Jane and Shirley exchanged worried looks and pulled the girls toward the stairs.

"I think you both should come upstairs now and take showers. You are filthy. Who knew that a trunk could be so dirty inside," Shirley added.

"No argument from us," Holly sighed in relief as she climbed the stairs with her mother, cousin and aunt in tow.

After they had showered, the girls sat on their beds and discussed what had happened to them.

"Something strange is going on here, Holly."

"I know. It was as if someone was sitting on the lid and keeping it from opening. Even my mom noticed that it wasn't that heavy to open and close once we were out."

"Our mothers both tried to open it when we were inside and had a difficult time. What does all this mean?" Abby put on her new thinking face.

"Do you think it has anything to do with that dust sprite that we discovered hiding in the books?" Holly tried out her own thinking face while looking in her hand mirror.

"Hmm, good question, Holly. We may have to have a meeting with our ghost friends and find out what they know. Something tells me they're not telling us the whole story about this dust sprite."

"I think you're right, Abby!"

***

Jane and Shirley were sitting in the kitchen and discussing the trunk over coffee.

"What's happening here, Shirl?"

"It was quite strange, Jane. I don't know what to make of it. The best thing we can do is keep the girls away from that trunk until we can figure out how to keep it opened."

"It frightened me to my core, Shirl. I don't want our girls going anywhere near it. Maybe we should get rid of it. I'll have Bob take it apart and fix it so it can't close completely. We know the girls won't stay away from it until they do a thorough search for whatever they are trying to find in there."

"I know. They're persistent. For now, we keep a close eye on them and make the basement off limits."

"Right! I agree! Phew, my heart is still racing. That was so scary. I should put something stronger in our coffee but I need to keep my wits about me to cook dinner."

"We can have a glass of wine with dinner or maybe two." Shirley smiled, sighed, and patted her sister on the back to put her at ease.

CHAPTER SEVEN

A Naughty Dust Sprite

The girls called out to Felicity and Minerva to discuss what had happened to them with the trunk.

Felicity was the first to float into the room followed closely by Minerva.

What's going on, girls? Are you okay? Felicity queried.

You both sound a little upset. Minerva added.

"Well, we are!" Abby exclaimed with emotion causing tears to bead up.

Oh no, what's wrong, Abby? Why are you crying?

"I'm not crying. I'm filled with emotion over what happened to us. I think you are holding back something about the sprite."

What are you talking about? What happened to you? Felicity circled the room in agitation.

"I'll tell you, Felicity, if you would please stop circling over my head. You're making me dizzy," Abby demanded.

So sorry, Abby. I'm feeling your stress and this is how I let some of my own stress off.

"Oh, I wish I could do that to relieve my stress," Holly exclaimed.

Minerva began circling around the room until she, too, was requested to stop.

"Minerva, please settle down and let me explain what happened."

Once the ghosts were settled against the wall Abby relayed the traumatic event with the trunk.

Felicity floated up and down and twirled around like a small tornado until she could talk.

I can't believe that! How awful for you both! Thank goodness your mothers were there to rescue you. If you are ever in need, all you have to do is whisper our names and we will come to help.

"But would you have been able to open the trunk? Our mothers had a difficult time lifting it together," Holly stated with a scowl.

Yeah, would we be able to lift something like that, Felicity? We are not strong in body since we no longer have bodies.

Felicity pushed Minerva's cloud aside and responded, *we can always find a way to get inside such things especially since we have no bodies. We can fit into almost any place. We would have found a way to save the girls.*

"Okay, thank you, Felicity. We will call if we ever need you. But what about the sprite? What are you not telling us about it?" Abby probed further.

Well, we didn't tell you that sometimes these sprites have a tendency to be naughty like little children. They look for ways to cause trouble. But don't worry about it. We will take care of this troublesome sprite.

"I hope so, Felicity. It caused all of us stress and scared us half to death."

"Oh, don't say death, Abby."

"Sorry, Holly. But if we hadn't been rescued…"

Don't even think that, Abby and Holly. We are here if you ever need us. You are safe. Now let Minerva and me go take care of this sprite before it gets into more mischief.

Before the girls could respond the ghosts had gone back to their hiding place in the passageways inside the walls.

"Well, I hope they can get rid of this pesky sprite. I don't want to deal with it again, Abby."

"Me neither. But we still need to explore the trunk. We saw something in there – something glowing. I need to get inside it again. But this time you have to stay out of it so you can open the lid in case it closes."

"Oh no, I don't want to go anywhere near that thing. You heard our mothers. It's off limits and a dead subject to them," Holly insisted. "And besides, I didn't jump in, you know. Something pushed me."

"I know, Holly, sorry. But we can wait until our mothers are asleep tonight and go down there."

"Are you kidding me, Abby? Go down to the basement in the middle of the night? It's creepy enough during the day."

"We have plenty of lights that Mom and Aunt Shirley brought down to use. What are you afraid of, Holly? We have ghosts in the house and you aren't afraid of them?"

"Well, that's true but we don't know what was down there. It could have been something other than the dust sprite. Maybe something more menacing even." Holly shivered at the thought.

Before the girls could discuss this more they hear Jane's voice calling them down to dinner.

"Let's go, Holly. I'm starving! All this discussion has made me hungry," Abby winked at her cousin as she raced Holly downstairs.

The ghosts in the meantime were busy hunting down the sprite to give it a piece of their minds.

CHAPTER EIGHT

Ghostly Advice

Felicity went directly to the library passageway and waited for the sprite to show up. After a few minutes, she instructed Minerva to go to the basement and check for the sprite there while I check here.

Minerva was nervous about meeting the sprite again. She didn't like what it had done to the girls. She knew it couldn't hurt her but it still made her wary of it.

Felicity called out, *Sprite, where are you? You know you have to come out sometime. We need to talk. Well, what I mean is, you need to listen.*

A cloud of dust flew in front of Felicity and stayed there.

Well, look who it is? Felicity called out to Minerva to come back upstairs.

You found it, Felicity! Now, what are you going to do with it? Minerva floated nervously back and forth.

I'm going to talk some sense into it and warn it to go away and not come back. Did you hear that sprite? If you understand what I said fly back and forth.

The sprite flew back and forth and stopped once again in front of Felicity as if waiting for more instructions.

You will not cause any more trouble for our friends, Abby and Holly. You will leave this house and go far away from here. You are not wanted here. Do you understand? Fly back and forth again to confirm.

The sprite flew back and forth and the next moment disappeared into the passageways leading to the chimney to escape.

It worked, Felicity. It's gone.

Yes, Minerva, I think it did. But I want to follow it to make sure it is gone for good.

Felicity swiftly flew to the chimney and followed upward to the top until she could see the sprite flying away into the clouds and becoming one with them.

Finally, it left, Minerva. We must tell the girls that all is well again.

Yes, let's go see them now. I like to see their smiling faces.

Minerva raced Felicity up to the girls' room to report the good news.

Hello girls. Well, you no longer have to worry about the pesky sprite. It's gone. You shouldn't have any more problems with it, Felicity reported.

"Thank you so much, Felicity. I don't know what we would do without you," Abby smiled with relief.

Holly sighed and said, "Thank you, Minerva. I'm sure you helped Felicity get rid of the sprite."

Oh my, thank you. I gave her my support by keeping an eye out for the sprite.

Holly smiled as Minerva swirled around in a circle as if she was dancing. The little ghost was clearly pleased that she had been given a compliment.

Abby poked Holly and asked, "Should we tell Felicity and Minerva what we plan to do later tonight?"

"Well, it's not definite that we are going to do that," Holly said with a quiver in her voice.

"I think my mom is going to throw away the trunk. This may be our only chance to discover what secrets the trunk holds."

What are you planning to do, Abby? Felicity flew up in front of Abby causing her to jump back in alarm.

"Why did you do that, Felicity?"

I'm sorry, Abby. But I don't think it's a good idea to go anywhere near that trunk. There could be something sinister inside it. I don't think it was the sprite that pushed you both inside the trunk. A sprite doesn't have that kind of power.

"I don't understand, Felicity. I thought you said the sprite causes mischief and all kinds of trouble."

It does, but it does not have any power to push someone into a trunk like that. I would feel better if you stayed away from the trunk until Minerva and I can check it over thoroughly.

I...don't know if I want to go near that trunk either, Felicity. What if it is a sinister spirit? It could harm us by sending us away. I don't want to leave the girls. I am happy here.

Oh, Minerva. You are a silly nervous ninny. Don't worry so much. I will protect you. No one is going to send you away.

Abby and Holly felt sad that they could not give the nervous ghost a hug to make her feel better. But it's difficult to hug a wisp of a cloud.

"Minerva, we won't let anything send you away. Only we can do that. Of course, we never will do that until you want to go on your own," Abby stated and blew her a kiss.

Thank you, Abby. I love you!

Abby giggled, "I love you too, Minerva."

"Me too, Minerva," Holly added.

Okay, you girls. That's enough of that silly mushy stuff. Come, Minerva, we have work to do. Oh, Abby, please stay away from the trunk until we tell you it's okay to go back to it.

"All right, Felicity. But don't take too long. I wanted to check it out tonight after our mothers are asleep.

The girls looked around but both ghosts had slipped away into the passageways without another word.

"That's strange, huh Abby?"

"Yes, but Felicity must know something about sinister spirits. We can give her some time. If we don't hear back from her by tomorrow night we go to the basement and search the trunk until we find something."

"Okay, Abby. But I want you to know that I don't like this idea at all," Holly sighed.

CHAPTER NINE

A Change of Plans

The girls kept busy part of the following day doing chores, and afterward, spending some time sunbathing in the backyard. It was a beautiful summer day.

They laid back comfortably on two lounge chairs sipping iced tea and talking over their plans to search the trunk that night. They hadn't heard back from the ghosts yet.

Jane and Shirley came out to see what the girls wanted to have for lunch.

"Hey, ladies of leisure. What would you two desire for lunch?" Jane laughed as the girls jumped up at the sound of her voice. They were deep in conversation.

"Oh, sorry, Mom. You startled us. We were busy talking and didn't realize you were standing there."

"No problem. I can put hot dogs on the grill or make some tuna salad. Which would you prefer?"

"Umm, either sounds good to us, right, Holly?"

"Sure, either one is yummy. Do you need help in the kitchen?"

"Okay, you can set the table outside since it's so nice out here. Put up the umbrella for some shade too."

"Okay, Mom. Come help me, Holly."

"Do you think she heard us talking about the trunk, Abby?"

"Na, I don't think so. She would have said something if she did."

Lunch was delicious but quiet. The girls didn't want to say anything for fear that they would talk about the trunk exploration that night.

"Why so quiet, girls?" Shirley asked.

"Um, we were busy eating. This tuna salad is delicious, Aunt Jane. Thank you!"

"Yeah, Mom, delicious!" Abby joined in giving her cousin a raised eyebrow in warning.

"You're welcome, girls. Why do I feel as if you are holding something back from us? Don't you think so too, Shirl?"

"Yes, I definitely think they are holding out on us."

"Come on, young ladies. Spill the beans. What are you up to?"

"Oh nothing, Mom," Abby responded with a serious expression.

"What about you, Holly? Do you want to tell us something?" her mother inquired.

"Oh no, I don't want to tell you anything. I…well…um…nothing."

Abby sighed and poked her cousin at her ineptness.

"You aren't planning to go to the basement and explore the trunk again, are you?" Jane smirked and winked at her sister.

"Well, um…I…" Abby couldn't say more. She sighed and hung her head.

"I knew it, Shirl. They were going to wait until we were asleep. Right, girls?"

Abby smirked and said, "Well, maybe a little, Mom."

Holly gasped in surprise that Abby admitted the fact. "I thought we weren't going to tell them, Abby?"

"Holly, it's okay."

"I told you that your father is going to look it over and fix it so it doesn't close. After he does that you can look inside again."

"When will Dad do that? We wanted to look inside again tonight."

"As soon as he gets back from his job later today. That's if he isn't too tired."

"Okay, Mom, we'll wait until that time," Abby sighed heavily.

Shirley and Jane suggested and smiled. "Girls, why don't we go to the beach tomorrow? We can pack a lunch and spend the day there."

"Sounds great, Mom!" Abby perked up.

"Yeah, sounds good to me too, Aunt Jane," Holly announced with a wide smile.

"Today we can take in that movie you two wanted to see about the dog," Shirley added.

"Great, Mom! We were wondering what we were going to do today." Holly winked at Abby.

"Why don't you girls clear the table and get freshened up. We will take care of the kitchen," Jane instructed.

"Oh, and check out the movie times," Shirley yelled up to the girls who had already gone up to their room.

"Sure thing, Mom," Holly answered back.

"Well, I guess that settles it. We can't go near the trunk today or tonight and maybe not tomorrow. Our mothers are keeping us busy."

"Yes, Abby. I noticed that. They have made plans for us for tonight and tomorrow all day."

"But that's okay. We'll have fun at the movies. I have been dying to see that movie about the dog's adventure. He is so cute!" Holly gushed.

"Yes, I agree, but I really did want to search the trunk some more. I hope my father doesn't decide to throw it all away."

"No, I don't think he will," Holly put on her thinking face. "Or will he?"

The girls enjoyed the movie in the late afternoon but couldn't stop thinking about the trunk and what would happen to it once Abby's father looked it over.

CHAPTER TEN

A Day at the Beach

The next morning the girls came down for breakfast. They couldn't wait to ask their mothers about the trunk.

Their mothers were busy preparing breakfast and their picnic lunch for the day at the beach. They were busy in conversation and didn't hear the girls enter the kitchen.

"What did Bob do with the trunk, Jane?"

"Well, he tried to lift the lid but couldn't open it at all. He hammered the top of the trunk but still couldn't lift it."

"Hmm, that's really strange?"

"We can't let the girls go near it until we can figure out what to do with it," Shirley stated.

"I agree, Shirl."

The girls stopped short at the kitchen door and listened in. They entered with a greeting.

"Good morning Mom and Aunt Shirley."

"Good morning, Mom and Aunt Jane."

"Oh, good morning, girls. How did you sleep?" Jane exchanged wary glances with her sister.

"Fine, Mom. We did hear what you said about Dad and the trunk."

"Oh, I see. Well, your father didn't have any luck in trying to take off the lid. He couldn't even open it."

"Does that mean we can't look at it again?"

Shirley answered this time, "Well, Aunt Jane and I have been discussing this and agree that it would not be a good idea for either of you to go anywhere near the trunk."

"Oh no, we have to look inside it one more time. There is something in there," Abby pleaded.

"Yes, I agree with Abby. There is something strange in there. It could be worth a lot of money too."

"What makes you think that, Holly?" Jane quizzed.

"Well, Abby said it was something glowing. It could be some antique jewels or something like that."

"Yes, we could be rich, Mom," Abby stressed.

"Well, I don't know about that. But if you go down there we have to be with you, right, Shirl?"

"Absolutely! You are not going down there by yourselves again, not after what happened."

"Okay, we can all go down there to search together. We may need help opening up the lid especially since Dad couldn't open it himself," Abby answered in serious mode.

"Don't look so intense, sweetheart," Jane smiled at her daughter to relieve the tension she was feeling.

"But first, girls, we're going to the beach. There will be plenty of time when we get back to go on a treasure hunt," Shirley announced and prodded her sister into finishing up their picnic lunch.

The girls sighed in disappointment but sat and ate breakfast without another word. They went upstairs after putting their plates in the dishwasher.

Abby and Holly picked out bathing suits, towels and cover-ups and slipped on their flip flops. They put on sunscreen, packed a change of clothes, books to read, and their iPods and went back downstairs.

"Are you all ready to head out, girls?"

"Yeah, Mom. We're ready," Abby smiled but not with her eyes.

Jane looked at her daughter's sad face and gave her a hug. "Don't worry, honey. We'll look at the trunk when we get back. We'll have a good time discovering what's in there together."

"Okay, Mom. Sure," Abby sighed again.

Holly picked up her beach bag and linked arms with Abby as they went out to the car. "It's okay, Abby. We'll find out what's in there later. But for now, let's have some fun at the beach. Okay?"

"Hmm, right, Holly."

The weather was beautiful, sunny and hot making for a jump in the cold water of the Atlantic refreshing until your toes curled up.

Before long the girls were jumping over the increasing waves and giggling like they were little girls again. They even saw some friends from school who were there with their families. Soon they were all jumping the waves together including their mothers.

Later they sat on the sand and built sandcastles with drips of the wet sand as turrets. The little ones who were close by watched in awe as the older kids created castles for them that would inevitably be destroyed by the oncoming waves.

It was soon time to take a break out of the sun, add more sunscreen and have some lunch.

The girls sat under the umbrella and helped their mothers spread out their picnic lunch. There was cold fried chicken, potato salad, homemade pickles, and fruit.

"Yum, this is so delicious, Aunt Jane."

"Yes, really yummy, Mommy," Abby giggled over her rhyming.

Jane smiled at Shirley and winked, both relieved to see their daughters having a good time and not tense anymore.

"Hey Mom, can Holly and I take a walk to the rocks and look for periwinkles?"

"Sure, make sure you have your cover-ups on and add some more sunscreen. The sun is pretty strong today without any clouds."

The girls nodded, added sunscreen and slipped on their colorful cover-ups. They met some other school friends who were also heading the same direction carrying pails for their collections.

Abby and Holly loved looking around the rocks for crabs, clams, mussels and their favorite periwinkles. The tide had gone out and now there were plenty of places to search. Before long their pails were full of loads of periwinkles. They looked forward to getting home to cook and enjoy these little delicacies.

It had been a long day at the beach but a fun and productive one. The girls dozed from time to time in the backseat as Jane drove them home. She and her sister whispered so as not to disturb the girls.

"What are we going to do about that trunk, Shirley?"

"I don't know. I think it's a menace to have around. It scares me half to death about the girls going anywhere near it again even if we are there with them. There is something evil about it."

"I know what you mean, Sis. But I promised them that we would go look inside it one more time. Maybe there is something in there of value. After we find it we can destroy the trunk once and for all."

"I agree. But we'll need Bob to help get it out of the basement. It's much too heavy for us to lift," Jane stated after glancing in her rearview mirror at the girls who appeared to be sleeping.

But were they?

CHAPTER ELEVEN

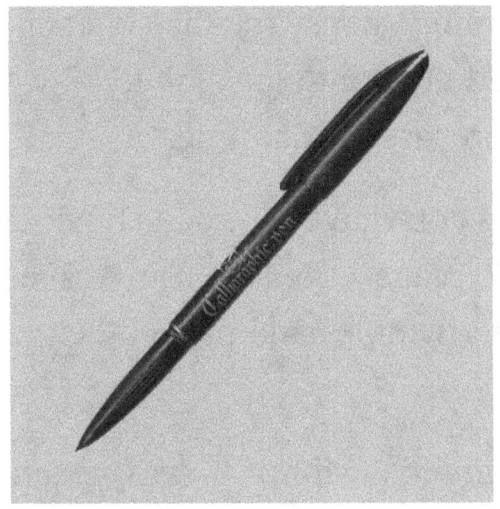

Another Disappointment

The girls were listening to their mothers' whispering and played along that they were still sleeping.

Once they arrived home they stretched and acted tired and sleepy as they grabbed their beach bags and pails full of snails that were in plastic bags of seawater. They carefully carried the brimming pails to the kitchen and placed them into the sink to be washed and prepared for boiling.

"Did you have a good time today, girls?" Jane asked as she washed out the periwinkles and placed them into a pan.

"Definitely, Mom! It was great! We got to spend time with some of our friends from school too."

"That's wonderful, Abby," Jane stated as she busied herself at the sink.

"You too, Holly?

"Yup, had a perfect day at the beach, Mom. Lots of waves, water, sand, sun, sandcastles and fun at the rocks exploring," Holly explained.

"We're going upstairs now to shower and wash our hair. We feel all sticky from the salt and sand. We'll put our bathing suits and towels in the wash for you."

"Thanks, girls. We appreciate that," Jane and Shirley smiled and nodded in unison.

"These periwinkles will be ready when you come back down," Jane announced.

"Okay," both girls said in unison.

***

"We have good girls, Jane. We're lucky to have them."

"I know, Shirl. We are fortunate."

"Let me help you clean up here. I'll put away all the leftovers and do the dishes. There's enough for another meal here, Jane."

"I know, I always make too much."

***

The girls took turns showering and sat with their hair up in towels to dry.

They couldn't wait to discuss what they heard in the car from their mothers' conversation.

"Do you think they will let my father destroy the trunk, Holly?"

"Hmm, I don't know. I think they must be curious after listening to us talk about jewels and riches."

"Yeah, but I think they are frightened about what happened to us. They don't want to keep it in spite of what we could find in it."

"Well, I still feel nervous about it myself. I thought we were going to…"

"Don't say it, Holly! I know. I was frightened too."

"Why don't we get the ghosts to help us? They said they were going to check it out. Maybe they did already. Let's ask them."

"Felicity, Minerva, where are you?"

Before the girls could blink, the ghosts were hovering in front of them.

"Oh, I never get used to your entrances, Felicity and Minerva," Abby exclaimed in alarm.

"Yeah, that is quite an entrance, ladies," Holly replied with a chuckle and a blanched face.

"They scared you too, Holly. I can see it on your face."

"Yeah, I guess a little."

What can we do for you, girls? Felicity spoke softly to help them catch their breaths after their fright.

Abby explained what their mothers had discussed about the trunk and her father's attempt to open it.

Well, that is strange indeed.

Minerva asked, *Oh oh, what caused that to happen, Felicity? Why couldn't Abby's father open it?*

I don't like this at all, Felicity audibly sighed.

"What does that mean, Felicity? Is it another ghost inside the trunk?"

Not a ghost, Abby. It is possibly a spell that was cast on the trunk. It is to keep anyone from touching something inside it.

"Well, we took out everything except a box. I saw something that was glowing coming from the box"

Was it shimmering? Did it move in waves?

"I didn't look at it too long before I was trapped inside with Holly."

"Didn't you both look the trunk over yet?"

Yes, we did look at it. But we couldn't get into it. I peeked through the keyhole and saw something at the bottom in a square box. But something was keeping me from getting inside.

I tried to get inside too. I'm a bit smaller than Felicity but still couldn't do it. There is something there. It appears to be a strong spell or entity.

The girls exchanged worried glances as they listened to their ghostly friends.

"What can we do at that point, Felicity?"

I don't think you should go near it. It could trap you in there, and even Minerva and I won't be able to get you out.

Oh my, please don't go near it. I don't want you to get trapped inside. I would miss you both.

"I don't believe it. How can that be? Who would have put a spell on a box inside a trunk? For what reason would there be to do such a thing?" Abby puzzled over this new development.

"I agree with them, Abby. I don't think it's worth the effort to try to get inside again. We could get trapped for good there," Holly's voice shook as she shivered.

"Wait a minute, Holly. Remember the books we found in the library with the fancy calligraphy writing? Let's look at them again. We might have missed something there about the trunk."

Abby pulled out the books she had tucked inside her nightstand while Holly searched for hers on her side of the bed. The girls brought the books over to the desk and laid them out for the ghosts to see.

Felicity floated closer and revealed her previous face in life to read it. Her long hair flowed around her serious face as she leaned into the books.

Minerva tried to do the same thing but could not bring up her life form and settled for her puffy little cloud as she looked over the books too.

The girls took a book each and perused through them as they did this in absolute quiet, not at all like their usual animated states.

A sigh could be heard from time to time out of the girls and at times from Felicity while the buzzing of bees could be heard coming from Minerva. These are the sounds that they have produced with permission from Meanna (Davey and Derek's Aunt Gigi's cat) and those on high to signify a sigh.

But, unexpectedly, other strange sounds soon were heard.

CHAPTER TWELVE

New Information

Suddenly two different sounds could be heard – a high C and a tinkling of a bell. The girls jumped out of their reading trances and looked at the ghosts who appeared to be amused as they swirled around the ceiling.

"What was that?" Abby inquired.

"Was that you two?" Holly asked.

Yes, the high C came from me and the tinkling of a bell came from Minerva. Did we startle you? That's how we laugh. Did you forget?

"Ha, yes, I guess we did, Felicity. Sorry about that," Abby chuckled.

"But what were you both laughing at?" Holly asked with curiosity.

Well, I read this book from a person who was living here before me. Her name was Annabelle. She said she put her jewels in a cigar box and stored them in a trunk in the attic, Felicity explained.

And I read another book, a diary, I think from another person, Priscilla, who said she put her jewels in a box in a trunk too. But she didn't say where the trunk was at that time. Strange, huh?

The girls' eyes opened wide and were at a loss for words.

"That means there could be lots of jewels in this box in this same trunk or that there may be another trunk in the attic," Abby said in excitement.

"We've never looked up in the attic, Abby? Can we go up there and check it out?"

"Well, my dad said he didn't trust the ceiling up there to hold us. He was going to work on it this past spring and make sure the roof was in good shape too. I don't think he got a chance to do that yet."

"So what can we do?" Holly said feeling dejected.

"We need to read these books from front to back for any other information we can find. Look how quickly Felicity and Minerva both found something of interest."

"Yeah, right. Let's get reading," Holly exclaimed.

Abby grabbed a notebook and took notes about what the ghosts had told them and jotted more notes as she read the books.

"These look like they are diaries from different people and times. Somehow they got put on the shelves in the library and were forgotten. That's where we found the dust sprite," Holly explained.

"Yes, each one tells of having something of value hidden in this house. Maybe something happened to their stash," Abby surmised. "What do you think, Felicity and Minerva?"

That's very possible, my friend. Even I had a couple of diaries but I don't know what happened to them. Oh...I think I stashed them in the passageways somewhere, Felicity announced. *I didn't want my mother or sister to find them.*

"Really, where do you think you put them, Felicity? Can you find them?" Abby asked in amazement.

"Yes, can we go search for them some time?" Holly inquired.

Umm, maybe someday. If I find them in the meantime, I'll let you know. Felicity swiftly floated out of sight into the passageways.

Minerva bounced up and down in a goodbye greeting to the girls and disappeared in a flash too.

"Boy, Felicity was in a hurry, Abby."

"I know. Maybe she's going to look for her diaries before we find them by accident."

"Yeah, I think she may not want us to read them, Holly."

"You may be right, Abby. Oh well, let's get back to these diaries. There's got to be something in here about a spell."

Abby picked up the two diaries that the ghosts had been looking over with some notes from Annabelle and Priscilla. The girls were only teenagers by the sounds of their daily activities.

"Look at this, Holly. These are Annabelle's notes. She said she swept all the floors on the third floor and afterwards had to wash them. She couldn't go to the party on the first floor that was going on at that time. This was when the house was used as a boarding house. They had entertainment down in the library with a piano. There is plenty of room to have one there now and lots of room to dance."

"Wow, Annabelle even drew a copy of the room with the piano and the furniture around the edges of the room with plenty of chairs to sit in between dancing. The curtains were dark colors and very ornate with long gold tassels," Holly exclaimed as she showed the drawings to Abby.

"Annabelle was talented and could have been an artist. I wonder if she ever did something with her talent."

Holly shook her head sadly. "No, unfortunately she never had a chance. She slipped and fell while washing the stairs one day. She wrote about her accident and she stopped writing. Look at the wet marks on this page. They look like tears. She said she could no longer walk and couldn't use her right hand to draw. It was also injured in her fall. That's why her writing is like a scrawl and uneven and the rest of the diary is blank."

"Oh no, poor girl. Maybe after that, she forgot about her jewelry and where she had hidden it. It no longer mattered to her," Abby sighed heavily.

"Yeah, Abby, who cares about jewels when you can no longer walk or do the things you once loved to do, like drawing."

"I feel so sad for Annabelle. I wonder if she ever got to have a boyfriend," Holly said in a trembling voice.

"I guess we will never know. She didn't write anything else in the diary. It's a blank after that last entry. Maybe she passed away shortly afterward," Abby stated.

Holly looked through the next diary and began to read about Priscilla, the other girl. She audibly gasped and held her breath.

"Abby, look at this! Priscilla wrote in her diary that she hated Annabelle and admitted to pushing her down the stairs. Evidently, she and Annabelle liked the same boy in school. The boy, Jeremiah, liked Annabelle though. Priscilla wrote that she did not want Annabelle to have Jeremiah for a boyfriend. She knew there was a party down in the library that weekend and somehow managed to get Annabelle in trouble with the owner of the boarding house. Thereafter Annabelle had to wash the floors and stairs on the third floor leaving Jeremiah without a dancing partner. This gave Priscilla an opening to pursue Jeremiah at the dance.

When Annabelle found out that Priscilla was trying to steal her boyfriend she was upset. They argued and Priscilla pushed Annabelle down the stairs.

Priscilla further states that when Jeremiah came looking for Annabelle the next day she told him Annabelle had moved away. Jeremiah left and never came back to the boarding house.

When Annabelle found out what Priscilla had done she put a curse on Priscilla and all her belongings that anyone who touched her things would be punished."

"Maybe that's why we got stuck inside the trunk. You touched the box and tried to reach inside," Holly announced.

"Right, Holly. I did try to reach inside but it stopped me and pulled me inside along with you."

CHAPTER THIRTEEN

Attic Search Plans

"How awful for both girls, Abby. They were only teens. I wonder if this Jeremiah was really a catch to warrant doing such a terrible thing."

"I can't imagine anyone being worth hurting another in that way. Poor

Annabelle. She lost everything in her life, her ability to walk, draw and her will to live," Abby exclaimed with vehemence.

"But also, Holly, look what Annabelle did to Priscilla. She put a curse on her and her belongings. She couldn't touch her own stuff I guess. That's why the jewels are still hidden in the trunk."

"But we don't know which girl's jewels are in the trunk in the basement and where the other girl's jewels are," Abby added.

"Unless we go searching in the attic." Holly grinned.

"Right, cousin, but we can't until we get the okay from my dad about the attic ceiling. We could have an accident and end up like Annabelle and never walk again. I don't want to take that chance. Do you?"

"No, I guess not. But maybe if we ask your father to help us."

"Hmm, that could work. Dad will do anything for me if I ask nicely and make him his favorite, chocolate chip cookies."

"Oh, nice, Abby. I love them too! I'll help you."

"It's supposed to be hot tomorrow so we will have to get up extra early to bake them before the sun comes up. Are you game for that, Holly?"

"Yup, I'll be up. Won't our mothers wonder why we are doing this? What do we tell them?"

"Well, we can tell them the truth that we want my dad to help us find something hidden in the attic. We were afraid to go up there ourselves for it could be dangerous. They will understand that."

"I bet they will, Abby. They don't want us down in the basement and now in the attic by ourselves."

"Now let's take a break from reading and pop some corn "and watch a movie," Holly begged.

"Yup, and I'll get out the licorice and candy bars for our snacks. I know how much you love candy and popcorn, Holly."

"I know, Abby. I can't watch without my popcorn and candy," Holly giggled and pulled out the jar of popping corn and the popper while Abby searched the cabinets for their candy stash.

The girls picked a few movies that they loved and drew straws for the one to watch. It was a superhero movie of course. They couldn't get enough of them.

"Leave some room for ice cream, Holly. I can't watch a movie without having ice cream during or after."

"We may not be hungry for dinner. Don't tell our moms we ate so much."

The girls snuggled together on the couch in the den/library with the big screen TV opposite the wall of books and snacked on all their favorites.

Their mothers were busy in the yard and hadn't noticed that the girls weren't there.

Shortly after eating all the junk food the girls sat at the kitchen counter and ate some ice cream, well, only a little sundae each as their mothers came into the kitchen.

"Well, look at this. The girls are having an afternoon treat. I like that idea, Shirl. Let's have some ice cream too."

"Sounds good to me, Jane."

The girls chuckled as their mothers joined them at the counter and made their own sundaes.

"What have you two been up to? We thought you were outside. We turned around and you two disappeared," Jane asked.

"Yeah, we had some reading to do, Mom. We also found out some interesting stuff in those books we found in the library. They were diaries of two young girls. We read a lot of them but there are more books to look through."

"What stuff did you find in them?" Shirley enquired.

Holly explained what they had found to her mom and also what they planned to do in their search.

Jane raised her eyebrows in surprise. "So, you are going up in the attic with your father?"

"Well, we plan to ask Dad when he gets home if he can go up there with us. It could be dangerous. Right?" Abby asked with a quizzical expression.

"Yes, it most definitely is not safe, honey. We don't even know what's up there. Your father has been so busy with everything else in the house. He was planning on doing that when it gets cooler. It gets terribly hot up in the attic in the summer."

"Oh, right. I didn't think of that. Sorry, Mom," Abby apologized.

"Well, I guess we will have to wait for a cooler day, Abby. That's okay. We can go to the lake tomorrow and hang out there with our friends."

"That sounds like a perfect idea, girls. We will go with you and pack a lunch. We can tell your dad and we can go to the seafood restaurant on the way home and of course visit your favorite ice cream stand. That's if you can possibly put more ice cream away, Abby."

"Of course, Mom. There is always room for ice cream," Abby chortled and looked relieved that the day wouldn't be a loss without the search. But her mind was already churning about what she would find up there in the attic.

CHAPTER FOURTEEN

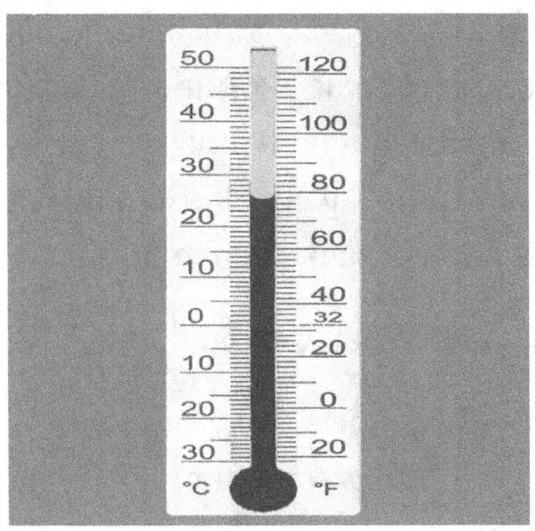

A Cool Summer Day

A few days later the weather began to cool down a little after a week of 90-degree temperatures. The girls had spent time at the lake and the beach and tried to stay cool inside on other days. They were getting restless and wanted to begin their search.

Today was the perfect day to begin. Abby's father was home and he had no other plans that morning. She found him in the kitchen fixing a couple of cabinets that were loose and doing odds and ends around the house.

"Hi, Dad. What are you doing?"

"Hi, Abby girl. How are you? I'm always finding something to fix in this old house. What's up?"

"Well, umm, I was wondering if you weren't too busy that you could help me with something."

"Sure, honey. What is it? Something needs fixing?"

"No, well, not really. I…Holly and I wanted to go up in the attic and search for a trunk or something. Can you go up there with us to make sure it is safe?"

The attic is located down the hallway from Holly's family apartment on the third floor with a pulldown ladder.

"Oh, Abby. I don't want you up there. It is not safe with the floor and ceiling. I need to check it over thoroughly first. I plan to get a guy out here to look over the roof too. But it's been so darn hot lately."

"I know, Dad. But Holly and I really need to look to see what's up there. Besides, it's a lot cooler today."

"Okay, honey. Let me get my flashlight and some tools. You'll have to stay at the bottom of the ladder until I can test the floor up there."

"Sure, we can do that. We'll wait until you give us the signal that it's safe."

Abby ran upstairs to get Holly and explain what her father had said. They both went up in excitement at a gallop to the third floor and waited at the base of the ladder going to the attic.

They listened as Abby's father tested the floorboards and tapped and nailed along the way. He called down to Abby and said, "Okay, honey. You can come up one at a time. I see a bunch of stuff at the corners and some furniture in the middle. What is it you are looking for?"

"Do you see a trunk or large box or something like that anywhere?"

"Let me get closer. Hold on a minute. Don't come up yet."

Abby stood at the top of the ladder and held on tightly as her father scanned the space with his large flashlight. She tried to see into the corners but it was too dark to make anything out. She did see a few pieces of furniture and some dark shapes in the corners as mentioned.

"Yes, there is a small trunk and a few larger boxes. They aren't too heavy. Let me bring them closer to you and you can look them over. We need to clear out all this stuff eventually. They could be a fire hazard."

Abby was shaking with anticipation as her father brought over the small trunk and several boxes. She grabbed the trunk and called down to Holly at the bottom of the ladder that she needed her help to get the trunk down the stairs.

"No, Abby. I will take them all down for you. I don't want you girls getting hurt trying to carry them down the ladder," her father stated emphatically.

"Okay, Dad. Let me go back down and you can hand them to me and Holly."

"Yes, that would work, Abby. Thank you."

Holly and Abby piled the boxes and the trunk at the bottom of the ladder and waited for Abby's father to come back down.

"Was that all there was up there, Dad?"

"Yes, honey. That was all the smallest stuff that I could handle for now. There are some bigger items, furniture and stuff. I need to have some men from work help me get them down. Do you want me to carry them downstairs to the library for you or are you going to open them up here?"

"Oh, right. Umm…can you carry them downstairs, Dad? That would be great. That way we can open them and easily throw away stuff we don't want."

"Thank you so much, Dad. Holly and I will make you a batch of chocolate chip cookies now before we open these boxes. They look a bit dusty and dirty."

"That would be great, Abby and Holly. You girls are the best. Happy I could help you out."

"We are happy you could too, Dad."

"Yeah, thanks so much, Uncle Bob."

"No problem, girls. My pleasure. I need to do a few more things around the house. Call me when the cookies are out of the oven. I love when they are hot and gooey."

Abby's Dad busied himself carrying the boxes down to the library and afterwards went back to doing his odd jobs around the house.

The girls whipped up the batch of 48 cookies as quickly as they could. They kept eyeing the boxes and trunk in the doorway of the library across the hall from the kitchen in between taking the cookies out of the oven. They were getting more excited as they finished cleaning up the kitchen and called Abby's father to try out the first hot cookie.

"Oh boy, these are delicious cookies, girls. Thank you so much. I think I will take a few more with me and have a cup of coffee with them. Thanks again. It's time for a break."

Jane and Shirley came in when they heard Bob say 'cookies.'

"Smells good in here, girls. What a nice surprise. It's time for our break too, Shirl. Let's get a coffee and have some cookies. Thanks, girls."

"You're welcome, Mom. Dad helped us and we wanted to say 'thank you.'"

"That's so nice of you both," Shirley exclaimed munching on a cookie.

"Did he go up in the attic with you?" Jane asked hesitantly.

"Yes, he did. But we waited on the ladder for him. He brought down some boxes and a small trunk. We're going to look them over now that we are finishing cleaning up. He said there are some more things up there and some furniture. He needs to get help from men at work to get them down."

"Okay. Go check out the boxes. I'll talk to your father about the other stuff. Great cookies, girls. Yum!"

The girls chuckled at their mothers enjoying the cookies as they brought the boxes and trunk closer to the couch and sat down next to them to begin their search.

Holly finished up her cookie and washed her hands of any chocolate before helping Abby begin their search.

CHAPTER FIFTEEN

A Valuable Find

With scissors in hand, Abby began to open up the boxes. They were taped down but the tape was dried and brittle making it easy to slice open quickly.

"Holly, let's open one box at a time. Okay?"

"Sure. Hurry up Abby, I'm getting nervous about this."

"What are you nervous about, Holly? Do you think something is going to jump out at us from these old boxes?"

"Well, I don't know…maybe." Holly sat back on the couch in the library and sighed.

Abby carefully pulled back the brittle tape and opened the cover. She reached inside and pulled out some dusty books and an assortment of handkerchiefs.

"What are those dusty rags for?"

"They are not dusty rags. Well, they are dusty but they're old fashioned handkerchiefs. They were used back in those days instead of tissues. I don't think tissues were invented yet. Look at the initials on them. Some have M on them and others have an F. Here are some with P and A. I wonder who they belonged to," Abby queried.

"Hmm, they were probably left by some of the inhabitants from years ago when this place was a hotel or boarding house," Holly responded thinking back to what Felicity had said when she had lived there.

Abby looked up in surprise and announced, "These could belong to Minerva and Felicity. Look at the initials – M and F. The A could be

Annabelle and the P could be Priscilla. I wonder why these handkerchiefs are all together in a box."

"I suppose they could be the phantoms' handkerchief. But maybe there were other people here that had the same initials," Holly surmised.

"We can ask the ghosts later, Holly. Let's look at the books. There's something else in here too."

Holly leaned in to get a closer look at what Abby was talking about.

"What is it, Abby?"

"Looks like magazines or newspapers and more books."

"Oh, anything else?" Holly asked clearly disappointed.

"No. Let's look at the books and the dates on the magazines and newspaper though," Abby added.

"Wow, Abby. Look - these are dated more than 100 years ago in 1885. Here is an old magazine, *Good Housekeeping*. I heard of that one from my mother. She said my grandmother and great grandmother used to read it. I don't think it's around anymore."

As the girls flipped through the newspapers they read out the headlines, *Nikola Tesla quits working for Edison*, *Mark Twain publishes The Adventures of Huckleberry Finn*, *Louis Pasteur uses first Successful Vaccine*, *Statue of Liberty arrives in New York*, *Ulysses S. Grant dies*, *Jumbo the elephant killed by a locomotive, and*

Grover Cleveland is inaugurated as 22nd President.

"This was really big news back in those days. I didn't realize there was an elephant named Jumbo," Abby laughed.

"Ha, you are funny, Abby. "That wasn't the biggest news. But imagine all these historic things happening way back then. Nothing much happens nowadays like that. All we seem to hear about are the bad things. Well, people are doing all kinds of good things to make the world a better place. We don't always hear about those things though, unfortunately," Holly sighed.

The girls read through the papers and were fascinated by all the history there.

They had almost forgotten about the books that were sitting at their feet and also the rest of the boxes and the small trunk.

They piled the newspapers, magazines back into the box to share with their parents later and picked up the dusty books.

Holly yelled out in excitement, "Oh my god, look at this book! We just read about it in the newspaper. It's *The Adventures of Huckleberry Finn*!"

Abby dropped the book she was looking at and leaned over to take a closer look at this find.

"This is incredible! It could be worth thousands of dollars to a collector. Is it in good condition?"

"Yeah, I think so. We need to dust the cover off," Holly answered with an awed expression on her face.

"Wait until we show this to our mothers. They will be shocked!"

"Let's put it on the table and open up the other boxes now, Abby. I can't wait to see what else is in them."

The girls were getting more excited as they opened up more boxes to find more newspapers, magazines and old hats and other clothes.

The last large box sat on the floor next to the small trunk. The girls were leaving the small trunk for last to make for more suspense.

The largest box was left, and they opened it together. The tape came off easily as did the others, but inside it, there was another box all taped up.

Abby reached in and lifted it slowly and placed it on the table next to the *Huck Finn* book.

"What do you think is in there, Abby?"

"Let's find out. The suspense is killing me."

"Yeah. Let's do it together on the count of 1...2...3," Abby announced.

The cousins pulled back the cover and jumped up in alarm.

"What is it?" Abby asked.

"Oh my!" Holly exclaimed.

CHAPTER SIXTEEN

A Shocking Find

"Oh no, I don't like the looks of this, Holly!"

"What...what is it?"

"I think it's an urn. You know what that means, don't you?"

"It's the remains of someone who died. Yuck! How disgusting!" Holly scrunched up her face in revolt.

"I know. Someone put it up in the attic. I wonder why?" Abby questioned.

"That is weird. Why didn't they bury it or something?" Holly shivered from shock.

"Well, it must have gotten packed up after the last people who lived here were gone. They forgot about it, I guess." Abby sat back and put on her thinking face.

"I suppose, Abby. But who is it?"

"Hmm. Let's see if there is a name on the urn," Abby said as she turned the metal object around and inspected it.

"Wait, I see some letters and numbers on the other side, Abby."

The girls wiped off the dust and read it out loud together, "Annabelle Bradley, Lived 1850, Died 1865."

"Oh no, Holly. It's Annabelle! She was only fifteen when she died!"

"Is there anything else in the box?"

"No, I already looked," Abby said sadly.

"I wonder if Felicity and Minerva knew her," Holly enquired.

"Yeah, we will have a couple of things to ask them now.

All that was left to do was open the small trunk. It sat at the girls' feet waiting to be opened.

"Well, I guess this is the last thing to open, Holly. Let's do it. Maybe this trunk will hold the answers to the diaries and the jewels that are missing."

The trunk was small enough to pry open with a letter opener since there was no key anywhere in sight taped under or on top of it.

Abby pulled out the letter opener from the desk nearby and twisted it in the lock back and forth careful not to break it. After several minutes a pop was heard indicating that she had breached the lock.

The girls exchanged worried glances and slowly lifted up the dusty green velvet cover.

They gasped collectively as they gazed down at several glittering pieces of jewelry that sat neatly in the small trunk or now jewelry case.

"Oh, look at these jewels, Abby! They are gorgeous! The stones are so big!" Holly gushed.

"How could a fifteen-year-old have all these jewels? It doesn't make sense."

"No, it doesn't, Abby. They can't be hers."

"I agree, but who do they belong to?"

"Good question. Well anyway, I think we found where the jewels were hidden. I wonder why they were never found," Abby asked.

"It could be that they were hidden behind the urn. I'll ask Dad where he found it upstairs. I don't think I would have wanted to go near the urn either if I had known it was up there." Holly's face pursed in disgust.

"Yeah right!" Abby agreed.

"What are we going to do with these jewels, Holly?"

"I don't know. Maybe we should ask our mothers. We could take them to a jeweler and see if they are valuable like the book."

"Yeah, that would be perfect. But we need to have our mothers go with us. We can't go into a jewelry store and expect them not to think we stole this stuff," Holly announced with concern.

"Oh no, that would be awful. Our moms will know what to do with the book and the jewels," Abby surmised.

"Right. Let's bring it up to our rooms with the book and look over the diaries again. Maybe we can discover who these jewels belong to."

The girls spend the rest of the morning and into the afternoon after lunch exploring the diaries. They called out to their ghost friends to help them with the discoveries.

CHAPTER SEVENTEEN

Questions Answered

"Felicity, Minerva, where are you? We need you," the cousins called out together.

The phantoms appeared swiftly as always in front of the girls. Abby and Holly took turns explaining to the specters about their precious discoveries and asked questions about what they had found.

Felicity spoke first, *To answer your first question - Did those handkerchiefs belong to me and Minerva? Yes, those are mine but not Minerva's. She never lived here, remember she was from the other old house in the neighborhood. The ones with A were Annabelle's and the M was probably Marietta's. The reason why the handkerchiefs are all together in a box is that we had a dance one night and each girl had to put her handkerchief in a box and the boys had to choose one. That is how they chose a dance partner. I guess we never got them back and they were stored away in the attic with all the other stuff once we were gone.*

As to the second question about the remains of Annabelle Bradley, she was already an occupant here when I arrived. She was a sweet girl and we were friends or we were beginning to be friends when suddenly she disappeared. We never heard what happened to her…but now I know.

"What do you know, Felicity? Do you know how she died?"

Hmm, not really but I may know who wanted her out of the way.

The girls exchanged shocking glances as they both looked back at Felicity in anticipation.

"Well, are you going to tell us or not, Felicity?" Abby queried anxiously.

Holly grabbed the diaries that they had been reading earlier and perused the pages. They suddenly noticed that there were more pages to read. They thought they had read them all.

"Wait a minute, Abby. Look at this. This page has wet spots on it and the ink ran and stuck the pages together."

"Yes, I see. The spots look like tears, don't they?" Abby announced unhappily. "Be careful pulling the pages apart."

"Yes, they do look like tear stains. She must have been upset about something," Holly stated sadly.

"Yes, she was. It says…"

At the dance, I danced with my new boyfriend, Jeremiah. We were sweet on each other. But I know there is another girl who also likes him. She was angry that Jeremiah was ignoring her.

Holly jumped off the bed and queried, "Was it Priscilla? We read about this love triangle."

Abby looked over her cousin's shoulder at the book that Holly held tightly in her hand.

Abby read the beautiful calligraphy, *I felt so happy in Jeremiah's arms as he twirled me around the dance floor. But I knew that her eyes were on us. She was so angry that her eyes were like black coals boring into my back.*

I didn't want her to ruin our evening so I didn't tell Jeremiah about her jealousy. He told me it was over with Priscilla and that he only loved me.

My dear friend Marietta said she would try to talk to Priscilla and make her understand that Jeremiah did not love her anymore.

I don't know if that will work.

Holly turned the page quickly to read the next lines.

On Sunday we went to church and I prayed harder than ever that Marietta would be able to convince Priscilla to find someone else. I am afraid of her. I think Priscilla wants to kill me. It may be the only way she can have Jeremiah all to herself.

"Oh my god, Holly! What if Priscilla killed Annabelle? She did, after all, push her down the stairs causing her injuries. But this fall had to have happened after the dance."

"That's possible, but how did she kill her?"

"We may never know. Felicity, what do you know about Priscilla?"

All I know is that she was here one day and gone the next right after Annabelle's disappearance. Her parents searched everywhere for her and never found her.

"Well, how do you explain why her remains were up in the attic?" Abby questioned further.

I can't explain that. But...Priscilla left the next day too. She said she was moving away with her parents. We never heard from her again either.

"What about Marietta? What happened to her?" Abby ventured further.

She dated Jeremiah and they eventually got married a year later. They were only sixteen. Some say Marietta may have been in love with Jeremiah for a long time.

"Really? Evidently, Annabelle and Priscilla did not know that." Holly said in a shocked voice. "They married too young, didn't they?"

"I guess they didn't know how she felt about Jeremiah. There was no mention in any of the diaries about that. Well, about marrying young in those days I think they married earlier," Abby surmised.

"Wait a minute. Why did Priscilla leave if she was the one who was jealous of Annabelle?" Holly quizzed.

I don't know. I didn't think too much about it at that time. I was upset with my own love interest. You know about that. It is too sad to talk about again.

"Yes, Felicity. You did tell us that. We were surprised to hear about your lost love. He was not good enough for you. For him to leave you after he told you he loved you and then go off and marry someone else. That was unconscionable!" Holly exclaimed.

Why did you have to bring it all back to me? Now I will have to go try to cry. You know it isn't easy for ghosts to cry. We are all dried up and have no tears.

It's okay, Felicity. Let's go. We can try to cry together.

Thank you, Minerva.

The specters flew out of the room and into the spaces of the walls to their special hiding places.

CHAPTER EIGHTEEN

A Secret Key

"I'm so sorry, Felicity," Holly whispered in apology to the ghost.

There was no sound heard. The girls sighed and went back to the diaries. Now that they knew more about the handkerchiefs they wanted to learn more about the girls involved.

The girls picked up the diaries again and read privately. Holly read from Annabelle's while Abby looked over the other books.

"Is there anything else in Annabelle's diary about Priscilla or Marietta?" Abby asked.

"No. But there is something glued inside the back cover of her diary. Look at this, Abby."

"Wow, it's a key. Maybe it's the one for her jewelry box that we opened already."

The girls jumped off the bed and raced to the desk where they had left the small trunk-like jewelry box.

Holly tried putting the key into the hole but it didn't work. She sat back on the bed and picked up the diary again looking over the pages for some mention of the key.

"Did you find anything about the key, Holly?" Abby probed.

"No. Maybe it's for another trunk?"

"What? Another trunk? Holly, it could be…oh my god! Yes…yes! Let's go see if it fits."

"Go where, Abby? What are you talking about?"

"You said it could fit another trunk. Didn't you hear yourself, Holly? The trunk is downstairs, remember?"

"Oh yeah! I wasn't thinking too clearly when I said it. Sorry. Let's go see if it fits."

The girls nearly tripped over each other to get downstairs. Once in the library, they slowed down before going down the hall to the door to the basement. Their mothers were out in the large kitchen/dining room busy banging pots and pans around so they didn't hear them.

The cousins tiptoed to the basement door and opened it slowly so it wouldn't squeak. They flipped on the one light for the bottom of the stairs and softly walked down the wooden steps to turn on all the lights that were left there previously.

They looked longingly at the large dusty brown trunk. But now it was looking newer than before. It was actually shiny and clean as if someone had polished it up. It even had some blue/greens tones in color amongst the gold and silver.

"Wow, it almost looks like new, Abby? Your father must have polished it clean."

"Yeah, maybe he did. I wonder if he tried to open it," Abby mused.

"Put the key in it, Abby. Hurry," Holly said excitedly.

Abby's hands were shaking as she got closer to the trunk. She touched the now shiny polished surface of the trunk which was quite beautiful. She could feel some heat rising up from within. It caused her to shrink back in alarm.

"What's the matter, Abby? Put the key into the hole," Holly stressed again.

Abby leaned closer and took a deep breath as she put the key into the hole and turned it. Much to her surprise, it opened with a soft click.

Holly smiled as she reached forward to lift the trunk. Just before her hand touched the gold and silver edge Abby pulled her cousin's hand back.

"Don't, Holly. Something isn't right. Can't you feel the heat? I don't know what could be causing it to be so hot. You could get burned. Let's go upstairs and get potholders."

Holly didn't wait to be told again. She raced upstairs and grabbed two sets of potholders under the watchful eyes of her mother and aunt.

"Hey, what's the hurry? Why do you need those, Holly?" her mother asked.

"We have some stuff to pick up that could be hot."

The mothers exchanged quizzical looks as they dropped what they were doing and followed closely behind Holly.

At the top of the stairs Abby waited and took one set of potholders from Holly and both headed back to the trunk.

Right behind the girls came their mothers who were concerned when they saw what the girls were going to do – open the trunk.

"Wait! What are you doing? That's too dangerous. Don't touch it!" Jane exclaimed in alarm.

Shirley pulled the girls away from the trunk before they could lift the lid.

Abby turned and cried out, "Why did you do that Mom and Aunt Shirley?"

"Don't you remember what happened the last time you did that? You ended up locked inside," Jane warned.

"I know but we have the key now, Mom. It can open it, break the spell and prevent anything like that from happening again."

"What makes you think that, Abby?"

"I just feel that it would work this time. We won't be in danger anymore, Mom."

"Yeah, I believe that too, Mom," Holly explained.

"I don't know about that, Holly. Your aunt and I are nervous about this trunk. We asked your Uncle Bob to get rid of it. Instead, evidently he cleaned it up."

Shirley looked at her sister with a questioning look.

"Umm, yes it looks like he did a good job cleaning it up. It looks quite beautiful in fact. Maybe we won't throw it away after all. But first, we must find out what is inside that is so interesting to you girls. Let's do it together."

The girls and their mothers shared one glove apiece and waited until Abby successfully turned the key and pulled it out of the keyhole. They carefully lifted up the heavy and hot cover and looked inside from a safe distance. They were still fearful of falling inside.

CHAPTER NINETEEN

Secrets Unlocked

The inside of the trunk was glowing with a bright blue light that was coming from the box at the bottom.

With a gloved hand and a firm hold of her arm by her mother, aunt and cousin, Abby leaned in and picked up the glowing box. It felt warm in her gloved hand. She carefully placed it on the floor and stepped back.

With the key still in her hand, Abby tried to open the locked box.

When it opened the foursome gazed inside at the glowing items as they oohed and aahed.

"Wow, look at those diamonds, emeralds, rubies, and sapphires. They are huge! Do you think they're real like the ones in the other box?" Abby asked in awe.

"What other box, Abby?" her mother questioned.

"Well, we were going to tell you about that too right after we opened this box, Mom," Abby stressed.

"Okay, I think we need to talk about this with your father. You may have discovered a treasure that is quite valuable. You say you have more like that in another box, Abby?"

"Yes, Mom. It's unbelievable, isn't it?"

"Yes, it is quite astounding. We need to put these in your father's safe in the library. Go get the other box too, girls. First we need to make an inventory of all the items in case someone is looking for them." Jane looked at her sister and rolled her eyes in amazement.

While the girls went upstairs to retrieve the other box their mothers looked over the gorgeous cache. They couldn't believe their eyes that anyone that young could have had that much valuable jewelry at that time. The stones were in old settings but still beautiful.

The cousins picked up the small jewelry box and also took along the diaries to show their mothers as proof of what they had found and how.

The four sat in the library on the couches and made their inventory. They had no idea how valuable the jewelry was and how wealthy they would be if no one claimed it. There were diamonds, rubies, emeralds, sapphires, tanzanite and other stones that they could not identify. There were more precious stones than they had ever seen at one time.

The girls shared the diaries where they had discerned the clues to find the jewels while their mothers read the passages that the girls pointed out. Jane and Shirley jumped up in alarm when they saw the urn with Annabelle's ashes.

"What should we do with the urn, Mom?" Abby asked in concern.

"Well, we could bury it with some of the money we obtain from the jewels as long as none of her family are still around and also if no one claims any of the jewels. Annabelle should rest in peace, the poor girl," Jane explained.

"Who is going to claim these, Mom?" Holly asked.

"Well, we don't know that yet. But we need to research the family of Annabelle since this looks as if it belonged to her. The other box that your father brought down from the attic could also be hers but we don't know that for sure," Shirley surmised.

"I think they are all hers somehow. Maybe she was given these by her mother, grandmother or another person. She knew they were valuable and that someone may try to steal them. So, she locked them away in the attic and in the basement away from everyone. She even put the key inside her diary and hid that away on the shelves with tons of other books. No one looked at the books evidently and therefore never found her diary until we did," Abby explained in excitement.

"It does make sense, that part anyway. But who would have that much jewelry to begin with back in 1885?" Jane exclaimed.

"Good question, Sis," Shirley agreed.

"Did you look over the other diaries to see if there was anything else about these jewels, girls?" Jane inquired.

"No, but we will keep looking them over," Abby answered.

The girls neglected to tell their mothers about a possible spell put on the trunk in the basement. Also that they suspected the jewels didn't belong to either of the girls.

"Well, you do that while we lock up the jewels and the urn until we talk this over with your father," Jane stated as she picked up the jewelry boxes, and headed over to the safe, at the other end of the room.

The girls looked over all the diaries for anything that hinted about who the jewels belonged to. They had almost given up finding anything until the last book.

Holly had it in her hand and cried out in surprise, "Oh, look at this, Abby! It says," *jewels were missing in some of the rooms on several occasions by occupants who stayed here. I didn't want to call the police because I think I know who is responsible. I must try to do something to stop her.*

191

"Whose diary is that, Holly?"

"Let me see. It looks like it says - Marietta."

"Oh no, does this mean that Annabelle is a jewel thief?" Abby cried out.

"Could be, Abby. Maybe Marietta found out what she was doing and killed her."

"Yeah, that means that Priscilla and is not the killer and maybe Marietta is. Right?" Abby sounded relieved.

"Who knows? We may never know who killed Annabelle, had her cremated, and placed in the attic," Holly said with a shiver.

"What else does Marietta say?" Abby inquired.

"Well, she talks about someone she likes but doesn't mention the boy's name. It looks like many of the pages have been ripped out after that. I wonder...Hmm. That is strange." Holly put on her thoughtful face.

"Stop thinking about that stuff. There isn't anything we can do about it now."

"I guess. But it is something to think about," Holly mused.

To get her cousin out of this mood Abby announced, "Do you know what this means, Holly?"

"No, what?"

"Well, we could be millionaires! Or at best hundred thousandaires. I think I made up that word. Who is going to be able to figure out who the jewels belong to after all this time?" Abby giggled in anticipation.

"That's right, Abby! Wow! Incredible!" Holly joined in with her own giggles.

Time would soon tell.

CHAPTER TWENTY

A Happy Ending

The cousins and their mothers researched the history of their Victorian home in the local library and contacted the historical society for any information about the background of their home.

They found that it was quite valuable in itself and that there were some things that they could not do to the house on the outside or inside without first checking with the society if they wanted to have it registered. It was too late though for some things that they had already done.

Several days were spent waiting for their lawyer to research the jewels and background of the former occupants of their old Victorian home.

They finally found out that anything that was discovered within its walls was now the property of the homeowner. No one had put in claims for any jewels or an urn.

They all sighed in relief as they took the jewels to a reputable jeweler where they discovered that they were now able to pay off their large mortgage and put money aside for college for both girls.

They made arrangements with their local funeral parlor to have the urn interned in a plot. The girls wanted to have a private ceremony for Annabelle in order for her spirit to be set free in peace.

The Mark Twain book was discovered to be worth over seven thousand dollars along with several other books valued in the hundreds. All in all, they were now owners of well over seven hundred and fifty thousand dollars.

Abby, can you believe this? We found a treasure inside our own house. Who does that?"

"It's so cool! Now we don't have to worry about working our way through college one day, Holly."

Their mothers were in the other room and heard what the girls had said.

"No, you will still have to work your way through but not at any old jobs. You will find something you like to do and do it to the best of your ability. No free rides here, girls," Jane explained with a chuckle.

"I think working makes for a better person, in the long run, girls. You need to know that you can't have it all that easily. There are many others out there who have to work hard for every little thing they have. We want you both to appreciate the little things in life," Shirley added.

Abby and Holly smiled and replied, "We do appreciate everything! We want to work even if we don't have to."

"I want to be an author. Having a little money will help to get someone else to promote me and my work one day," Holly exclaimed.

"You will be rad, Holly! I, of course, will be a fabulous fashion designer one day. We will both be famous in our professions in the future."

"Yeah, we can only hope, Abby. We will do our best at whatever we plan to do. In the meantime, nothing is going to change. Our parents will make sure of that. We still need to do our chores and earn our allowance. No free rides here!"

"You got that right, Holly."

"Hey Mom, are you going to call Dad to tell him about this? He won't believe it!" Holly exclaimed.

Holly's dad, Jaye Lester, is a doctor who travels with Miracles Across Borders and cares for the needy in other countries. Her mother, Shirley, is a registered nurse. She was working with her husband until she got sick from her diabetes and had to leave the group. Jaye still had some time left on his contract to complete.

"Well, I guess I could, Holly. I'll go out to the kitchen and call him now," Shirley announced as she left the room.

"Wait a minute, Mom. I want to talk to Dad too," Holly yelled and followed after her mother to get her attention.

Shirley finally got in touch with her husband after waiting for several minutes for him to pick up. He had been at the hospital caring for a patient.

"Hi, Shirl. How are you and Holly doing? I've been meaning to call you but it has been so hectic here. We are short-staffed again. Some of the doctors left to go to another hospital."

"Oh, sorry to hear that, Jaye. We are doing well. I wanted to tell you about some new developments here at my sister's house. It's quite astounding."

Shirley recapped all the discoveries and how much it all was worth. She also told him about their apartment that Bob had finished and how wonderful he had been to do so much for them without compensation.

Jaye surprised Shirley by responding, "Well, I guess we won't have to pay him for all the work he did now since he is quite rich," he laughed.

"Well, I guess he won't want to take anything for it but I would definitely offer him something for all his work," Shirley retorted, sadly disappointed in her husband's cavalier attitude. She added, "Do you know when you will be coming home?"

"I won't be coming home for a while yet, Shirley. In fact, I don't know when I will be able to get away."

"Oh, I see. Well, we'll talk again soon. Holly wants to talk to you now," Shirley stated in a subdued and sad voice as she handed over the phone to her daughter.

"Hi, Dad. How are you? I really miss you. Mom told you about our discoveries. Can you believe it? It's so cool, isn't it? We're all rich now."

"Well, your Aunt Jane and Uncle Bob and cousin are rich, not you. Sorry to burst your bubble, honey."

"Oh...um...yeah. I guess. When are you coming home, Dad?"

"I don't know, honey. I'm really busy and we are short-handed here at the hospital. I will call if and when I can make it. Okay? Say goodbye to your mom. I love you, Holly."

"I love you too, Dad. Bye."

Shirley was sitting at the table with her head down on her folded arms when Holly came over to give her the cell phone.

"Are you okay, Mom? Is everything all right with Dad?"

"Sure, honey. Everything's okay. I'm just tired after all this excitement. Why don't you go upstairs and get cleaned up? We will be going out in a couple of hours. I know how you and Abby like to get prettied up for the boys."

"Okay, Mom. See you in a little while."

Shirley didn't want her daughter to see the tears that were threatening to fall. She grabbed some tissues from the bathroom nearby and blew her nose. As she turned to go back to the library her sister was there watching her.

"What happened, Shirl?"

"I don't want to talk about it now. This is a time for celebration. There will be time to discuss this later. Okay?"

"Are you sure? I am here if and when you need me. Now let's get cleaned up. We have some celebrating to do, Sis!"

"Sure. We'll have time to talk later. Let's celebrate!" Shirley smiled wanly.

Jane patted her on the back and hugged her as they both headed up to their bedrooms to change.

Jane dialed her husband as she got ready. "Hey, honey. How are you? Are you getting home soon?"

"Hi, sweetheart. Yes, I was just getting ready to leave. Is everything okay?"

"Oh, everything is more than okay," Jane announced with glee. She explained everything quickly and laughed at Bob's exclamations of amazement and gasps to get his breath.

"Is this for real, honey? This isn't April Fool's Day or anything?"

Jane giggled, "No, of course not, Bob. This is the real thing. Can you believe it? We are going to be rich!"

"Ha ha, we are already rich! We need to go out and celebrate."

"Already planned, honey. Get home so we can begin the celebrating."

"Will do. Wow, what a strange ending to this day. Strange but definitely good!" Bob laughed and headed out to his car looking forward to getting home.

***

They were still riding on cloud nine with all the secrets this house kept giving up. They planned to go out to the Italian restaurant, Piccolo Italiano, that night to celebrate in style with plenty of chicken, veal and eggplant cutlets, meatballs, spaghetti and salad. The girls' good friends, twin detectives, Davey and Derek, had told them about Piccolo. It had become the girls' favorite Italian restaurant too.

The cousins called Davey and Derek, to share their news and fabulous discoveries. They talked excitedly to them for about an hour.

The boys agreed that the girls' house was the most awesome house ever. Who knows how many more secrets there were yet to be discovered?

Abby and Holly asked the boys, "Do you and your family want to join our families for a celebration dinner at our favorite Italian restaurant tonight?"

The girls had been given permission ahead of time to invite their friends and family out to help celebrate with them.

"Really? Wow, that's cool. I love Italian food at Piccolo and so does Derek and the rest of the family. It's our favorite restaurant. I'll ask Mom. Hold on a minute, Abby."

Davey raced off to find his mother in the kitchen before she could start dinner. He was back in a jiffy with a positive answer for Abby.

"That's great, Davey! We are all so excited about this. I still can't believe it! Who would have thought that a young girl of fifteen years would be a jewel thief?"

"Yeah, I know. But what if she didn't do it? Maybe someone else did and hid the stuff in those boxes and forgot about them or maybe died."

"Hmm, that's interesting to think about, Davey. You are the detective after all. Maybe one day we will discover who did it. Also, I want to know how Annabelle died and why her urn was in the attic. That is a mystery to solve. Maybe one day we will know."

"Well, if you and Holly need any assistance, I know two detectives who will work on the case," Davey laughed.

Derek was listening to his brother on his end while Holly was listening to her cousin on the other. They all were chuckling after everything being said was explained.

"Well, see you guys later at the restaurant. My mom made reservations for 7:00 pm. Can't wait to eat some cutlets! Yum!" Abby exclaimed as her mouth began to water.

Holly sat down on the couch and sighed, "What do you think you should do with all the money, Abby? My father said that it was not my money to decide how to spend it."

"You are part of this family, Holly. What is ours is yours, too. Well, my parents said they want to give some to charities, the schools and the local food bank. They said there are so many people who need help."

"I agree, Abby, about giving some to charities but I don't think I should have any of the money since it was found in your house."

"No, I disagree, Holly. You were instrumental in helping me find it. You deserve a share too."

"Thanks, Abby. I appreciate that. But our mothers already said they were going to use some for college for us. I will be getting my share that way."

"Don't worry about anything, Holly. I will take care of you.'

"Thanks, Abby. I love you."

"Hey, don't go crying now. I love you too."

"Well, we better get ready for dinner. We're going to see the twins and must look our best."

"Right! Hurry up. Let's get going. I'm starving!" Abby raced ahead up the stairs.

"Wow, it's been a crazy summer so far, Abby."

"I know. We have lots more stuff to do and many more discoveries to make in this old house. Can't wait to uncover some more secrets."

"I'm ready if you are, Abby!"

THE END

A NOTE FROM THE AUTHOR

Watch for Book 4 in this series coming in late 2019 or early 2020!

Thank you for purchasing one of Jemsbooks. If you like this book, a review would be greatly appreciated wherever you purchased it. Word of mouth is the best way to spread word of books. Please share your review with friends and family. I would love to hear from you about my books.

Please go to my website for mo http://www.jemsbooks.com.

All my books are available on Amazon and Barnes & Noble.

This is the third book in this middle-grade series. I plan to write a few more of these books in the next year or two.

In this book, I touch on handling unexpected incidents and how to overcome disappointments in life.

The themes in all Jemsbooks deal in life lessons and teaching children how to be polite, kind, and sensitive to others' feelings. We need to remind children of all ages to treat one another with respect and kindness.

I want children to know that it's okay to be different. It is extremely important that all children feel safe and loved in their homes and in their lives.

I hope your children will enjoy these entertaining and fun stories and learn valuable lessons that will stay with them for a lifetime.

Look for more books in this series and the Davey & Derek series coming in 2020, and a YA fantasy series coming in 2020 and 2021 and beyond.

With Blessings & Love,

Janice Spina

ABOUT THE AUTHOR

Janice Spina is a retired administrative secretary from a public school system in Massachusetts. She has always loved writing poetry and children's stories.

This is the third book in this middle-grade series. Janice has published 12 children's books for Preschool-Grade 3, six books in a middle-grade detective series for boys, three books in the middle-grade Series for girls under Janice Spina and three novels and a short story collection under J.E. Spina. She continues to write more children's books and is in the process of editing more books for publication.

Janice's books have received 14 Book Awards and three finalists – one Mom's Choice Award, 10 Pinnacle Book Achievement Awards, two from Reader's Favorite Book Awards – Honorable Mention and a Silver Medal, and a Silver Medal from Authorsdb Cover Contest and two books were Finalists in Authorsdb First Lines Contest and another one a Finalist in Red City Review Book Awards.

Janice loves to hear from readers and fans and will share your reviews on her blog if you contact her at jjspina@comcast.net

Look for more Jemsbooks on her website

http://www.jemsbooks.com

Amazon Author Page for all Jemsbooks:
http://amazon.com/author/janicespina7

Follow her on:

Twitter: http://twitter.com/janice_spina

Facebook Main Page:
http://www.facebook.com/janice.spina.9

FB Author Page:
http//www.facebook.com/janicespina7

FB Novelist Page:
http://www.facebook.com/jespina77

She also has a blog:
http://www.jemsbooks.blog

Janice lives in New Hampshire with her husband, John, who is her illustrator/cover creator, and two aquariums of fish – one saltwater and the other freshwater.

Janice's slogan is: ***Reading Gives You Wings to Fly! Soar with Jemsbooks.com all year through!***

Happy reading! Reading is good for your health!

ABOUT THE ILLUSTRATOR

Dr. John Spina is a retired elementary and middle school principal from a public school system in Massachusetts. John has a doctorate in Educational Administration.

John has illustrated and created covers for 12 children's books for PS-Grade 3, and six books in the *Davey & Derek Junior Detectives Series*. This is the third book in this middle-grade series he has illustrated.

He has also created the covers for Janice's three novels, *Hunting Mariah, How Far Is Heaven, Mariah's Revenge,* and a short story collection, ***An Angel Among Us,*** all of which she wrote under J.E. Spina.

He is currently working on illustrating more of Janice's books and covers in between being the caretaker of their two tanks of fish, one tropical and the other freshwater.

Their joint goal is to encourage children of all ages to read.

Reading has been documented to be good for your health. Happy Reading!